D1177469

SARA AND THE DOOR

VIRGINIA ALLEN JENSEN

drawings by Ann Strugnell

▲▲Addison-Wesley

Library of Congress Cataloging in Publication Data
Jensen, Virginia Allen.
  Sara and the door.
  SUMMARY: While trying to free herself from the
front door, Sara learns about buttons.
  [1. Stories in rhyme]   I.   Strugnell, Ann.
II. Title.
PZ8.3.J425Sar   [E]   76-28987
ISBN 0-201-03446-8

Sara closed the door
all by herself.

But she closed it on her coat,
and she couldn't pull it out.

What could Sara do?

The knob was too high
for Sara to reach.

What could Sara do?

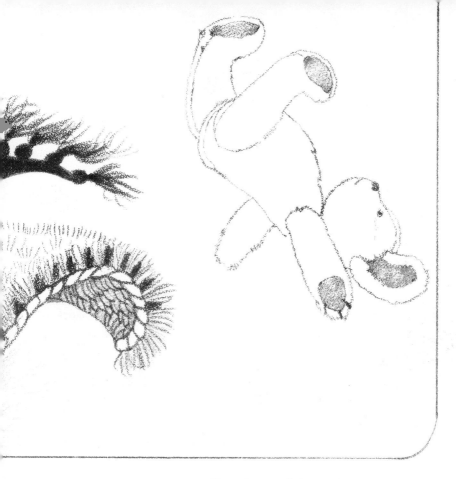

She stooped down
to slide out of her coat,
but she was stuck in that, too.

She called for help
but no one came.

So she stood up
and looked all around.

Nobody there . . .
no one around.
What could Sara do?

She closed her eyes
and then shook her head.

She would still be there
when it was time for bed.

Tears rolled down
cold on her cheeks.

They fell on her coat
and on the buttons, too.

Buttons. Buttons!

That's what she'd do.
Undo the buttons
all by herself.

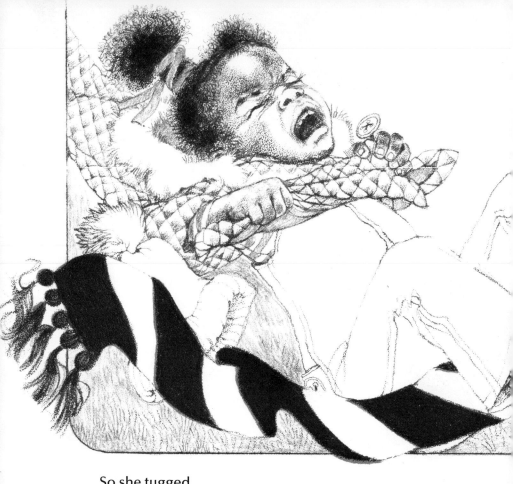

So she tugged
and she pulled
and she pushed

and she yanked,
but they wouldn't
come off.

Then she saw some holes
to push the buttons through.

So that is what she did
with button one
and button two
and three.

Sara turned around
and pulled off her coat
and finally walked away.

For Sara this was
a very satisfying day!

Virginia Allen Jensen grew up in the Midwest but now lives in Denmark with her husband and children. The author of many children's books, she has a special fondness of *Sara* because it grew out of an incident that actually happened to her daughter, Kirsten, now 6' 2" and better able to manage doorknobs.

Ann Strugnell, a young British artist, found her Sara while visiting Boston, Massachusetts, in the summer of 1975. Ann went sketching in Fenway Park, and a small girl across the field was her first subject. "It seemed just right to use those sketches for the first American book I was commissioned to illustrate. *This* one."